The Three Little Pigs

WRITTEN BY
VIVIAN FRENCH
ILLUSTRATED BY
LIZ MILLION

WALKER BOOKS
AND SUBSIDIARIES
LONDON • BOSTON • SYDNEY

First published 2001 by Walker Books Ltd
87 Vauxhall Walk, London SE11 5HJ

2 4 6 8 10 9 7 5 3

Text © 2001 Vivian French
Illustrations © 2001 Liz Million

This book has been typeset in Cygnet Demi Bold.

Printed in Singapore

British Library Cataloguing in Publication Data
A catalogue record for this book is
available from the British Library.

ISBN 0-7445-6898-6

Notes for Children

The Three Little Pigs is the story of a family of
pigs and a big bad wolf.
You may know the story already, but it doesn't
matter if you don't.

This book is a little different from other picture books.
You will be sharing it with other people and telling
the story together.

You can read

this line

this line

this line

or this line.

Even when someone else is reading, try to follow
the words. It will help when it's your turn!

"I'll huff –"

Huff! Huff! Huff!

"And I'll puff –"

Puff! Puff! Puff!

"And I'll blow your house down!"

CRASH!

Who said that?

The wolf said it!

The wolf?

What wolf?

The big wolf.

The big bad wolf.

The big bad hungry wolf.

Huff! Huff! Huff!

Why did he say it?

He was hungry.

He wanted to eat the little pigs.

What little pigs?

Yes, what little pigs?

There were three little pigs

And they lived with their mum.

They lived in a pig sty

And they grew bigger

And bigger

And bigger!

One day their mum said,

"You're too big!

Too big for the pig sty."

Their mum said,

"It's time you had houses of your own."

So off went the three little pigs.

The first little pig met a man

A man carrying some straw.

And the little pig said,

"Please can I have some straw?"

And the man said, "Yes."

So the first little pig built his house

And he lived there happily

Until –

Along came the wolf!

The big bad wolf.

And the wolf said,

"I'll huff –"

Huff! Huff! Huff!

"And I'll puff –"

Puff! Puff! Puff!

"And I'll blow your house down!"

So he huffed –

Huff! Huff! Huff!

And he puffed –

Puff! Puff! Puff!

And he blew the house down!

CRASH!

And he ate the first little pig all up.

Munch! Munch! Munch!

Crunch! Crunch! Crunch!

No he didn't.

Yes he did.

No he didn't!

The first little pig ran

And he ran and he ran.

Where did he run?

To the stick house.

What's that?

What's what?

What's a stick house?

A house made out of sticks.

Who made it?

The second little pig.

How did he make a stick house?

He met a man

A man carrying some sticks.

And the second little pig said,

"Please can I have some sticks?"

And the man said, "Yes."

So the second little pig

Built his house out of sticks.

Was it a big house?

It was a pig house!

Then along came the first little pig –

EEEK! EEEK! EEEK!

"Let me in!

Let me in!"

So the second little pig let him in

And the two little pigs

Lived happily together

Until –

Along came the wolf!

The big bad wolf.

And the wolf said,

"I'll huff –"

Huff! Huff! Huff!

"And I'll puff –"

Puff! Puff! Puff!

"And I'll blow your house down!"

So he huffed –

Huff! Huff! Huff!

And he puffed –

Puff! Puff! Puff!

And he blew the house down!

CRASH!

And he ate both the pigs.

Munch! Munch! Munch!

Crunch! Crunch! Crunch!

No he didn't.

Yes he did.

No he didn't!

The little pigs ran

And they ran and they ran.

Where did they run?

To the brick house.

I know who lived there.

Who?

Was it the wolf?

No!

It wasn't the wolf.

It was the third little pig.

That's right.

Did she make her house too?

Yes she did.

How did she make it?

She met a man—

I know what he was carrying!

What was he carrying?

Bricks!

And the third little pig said,

"Please can I have some bricks?"

And the man said, "Yes."

So the third little pig

Built her house out of bricks.

Then along came

The first little pig!

And along came

The second little pig –

EEEK! EEEK! EEEK!

"Let us in!

Let us in!"

So the third little pig let them in

And the three little pigs

Lived happily together

Until –

Along came the wolf!

The big bad wolf.

And the wolf said,

"I'll huff –"

Huff! Huff! Huff!

"And I'll puff –"

Puff! Puff! Puff!

"And I'll blow your house down!"

So he huffed –

Huff! Huff! Huff!

And he puffed –

Puff! Puff! Puff!

And he blew the house down!

CRASH!

No he didn't.

Didn't he?

No – it was a brick house.

A house made out of bricks.

The wolf huffed

And he puffed

And he huffed and he puffed

And he puffed and he huffed

But it was no good.

No good at all.

So he climbed and he climbed –

Huff! Huff! Huff!

Up onto the roof –

Puff! Puff! Puff!

And up to the chimney.

What did he do then?

He slid down the chimney.

And he landed …

SPLASH!!!!!

In a pot of water.

Was it hot water?

Boiling hot water!

OW! OW! OW!

And that was the end.

The end of the wolf.

The big bad wolf.

And the end of the story.

No more huffing!

No more puffing!

I know the proper ending.

So do I.

What's the proper ending?

The three little pigs

Lived happily ever after!

Notes for Teachers

Story Plays are written and presented in a way that encourages children to read aloud together. They are dramatic versions of memorable and exciting stories, told in strongly patterned language which gives children the chance to practise at a vital stage of their reading development. Sharing stories in this way makes reading an active and enjoyable process, and one that draws in even the reticent reader.

The story is told by four different voices, divided into four colours so that each child can easily read his or her part. The blue line is for more experienced readers; the red line for less experienced readers. When there are more than four children in a group, there is an ideal opportunity for paired reading. Partnering a more experienced reader with a less experienced one can be very supportive and provides a learning experience for both children.

Story Plays encourage children to share in the reading of a whole text in a collaborative and interactive way. This makes them perfect for group and guided reading activities. Children will find they need to pay close attention to the print and punctuation, and to use the meaning of the whole story in order to read it with expression and a real sense of voice.

The Big Book version can be used to introduce children to *Story Plays* in shared reading sessions. The class can be divided into groups to take part in reading the text aloud together, creating a lively performance.